P9-DFU-314

The Branch

Written by Mireille Messier
Illustrated by Pierre Pratt

Kids Can Press

It's past my bedtime, but I can't sleep.
Maybe it's because I'm too excited about the holidays.
Maybe it's because of the sound of the icy rain hitting my window.
Tik! Tik! Tik! Tik!

When I finally doze off, I dream that I am wearing a crown of icicles. My tree is my castle. My branch is my throne. I am Queen of the Storm!

Creak!
Crack!
Crash!

My eyes snap open.
What's that noise?
I throw back my covers
and rush to the window.

Everything outside is covered in ice. It looks like the entire neighborhood has been wrapped in a heavy blanket of diamonds. It's beautiful. But a little scary, too.

Mom stands next to me at the window. Her breath makes a cloud on the glass.

"We're lucky the whole thing didn't come down!" she says.

"What came down?" I ask.

That's when I see it.

At the foot of my tree lies a big broken branch.

I rush down the stairs and out the door.

That was the branch I sat on, jumped from, played under.

It was my castle, my spy base, my ship ...

I try to pick up my branch, but it's too heavy.

I run my fingers along the bumpy ice.

"Can we fix it?"

"I'm afraid not," says Mom.

"Can I keep it?"

"It's just a branch ..."

"It's not just a branch to me! I played on this branch all the time!"

Mom touches the splintery part on the trunk where the branch used to be.

"All right. You can keep it for a little while."

"But I want to keep it forever."

"We'll see," says Mom, squeezing my hand.

I know that squeeze. It means "probably not."

As I look around, I see more broken branches — in the yards, in the street, stuck upside down in the trees. I watch my neighbors digging and scraping. They gather broken branches and carry them to the curb, making big heaps. Like beaver dams in the city.

Workers in shiny coats are clearing the road. They climb ladders, fix wires, wrap yellow tape around trees and put orange cones on the sidewalk. Everybody is so busy. I wish I could climb my tree to watch them. But I can't.

My next-door neighbor, Mr. Frank, is out
with his chainsaw. The buzzing makes my
ears ache. But I won't go back inside. I block
my ears and guard my branch. I want to
make sure nobody comes to take
it away or chop it up.

Finally, Mr. Frank stops sawing when he catches sight of me over the fence.

"Why the long face?"

"My favorite branch broke."

"Oh! I see. So, what are you going to do with it?"

I shrug. "It's just a branch ..."

"Just a branch? But it was your favorite, right?"

I nod.

"That's what I thought. That branch is full of potential!"

"What's *potential?*"

"It means it's worth keeping."

Mr. Frank hands me a small piece of wood.

"What do you see?"

"A piece of wood ..."

"Sure. But what could it become?"

Mom comes over, carrying mugs of hot chocolate.

"Hi, Frank! I see part of your tree came down, too."

"Yup. That was quite a storm we had."

"We're guessing what's hiding inside the wood," I tell Mom.

Mr. Frank chuckles at Mom's puzzled look.

"I build things from salvaged wood," says Mr. Frank. "With some imagination, each broken piece can become something great!"

I look at my favorite branch. It has potential.

I concentrate. I squint. And then, I have an idea!

"I know what my branch can become!"

"I knew you would," says Mr. Frank.

"What is it?" asks Mom. "Is it a walking stick? A coatrack? A birdhouse?"

"No. It's even better!" I say.

I cup my hand and whisper into Mr. Frank's ear.

"Oh! Good idea!"

"But I don't know how to make it."

"I can help," says Mr. Frank. "I have the tools and I have the time. All you need is elbow grease."

Mr. Frank's workshop smells sweet, like Sunday breakfast. We work together on weekends and sometimes after school. He shows me how to use the tools to make my branch into something new.

We draw plans.
We measure.
We saw.

We saw
some more.
We dry the wood ...
then we wait ...
and wait ...
and wait ...

We plane.
We make holes.

We sand.
Then we varnish — three coats,
to make it last a long, long time.

It wasn't just a branch. It was my branch. The one I sat on, jumped from, played under. It was my castle, my spy base, my ship ...

It still is!

To Albert, our tree — M.M.

Kids Can Press acknowledges the financial support of the Government of Ontario, through the Ontario Media Development Corporation's Ontario Book Initiative; the Ontario Arts Council; the Canada Council for the Arts; and the Government of Canada, through the CBF, for our publishing activity.

Published in Canada by
Kids Can Press Ltd.
25 Dockside Drive
Toronto, ON M5A 0B5

Published in the U.S. by
Kids Can Press Ltd.
2250 Military Road
Tonawanda, NY 14150

www.kidscanpress.com

Edited by Yasemin Uçar
Designed by Julia Naimska

This book is smyth sewn casebound.
Manufactured in Shenzhen, China, in 3/2016 by C & C Offset

CM 16 0 9 8 7 6 5 4 3 2 1

Library and Archives Canada Cataloguing in Publication

Messier, Mireille, 1971–, author
The branch / written by Mireille Messier ; illustrated by Pierre Pratt.

ISBN 978-1-77138-564-0 (bound)

I. Pratt, Pierre, illustrator II. Title.

PS8576.E7737B73 2016 jC813'.54 C2015-907225-5

Kids Can Press is a Corus™ Entertainment company